Spiderwort and the Princess of Haiku

J. H. Sweet

Illustrated by Holly Sierra

What follows is the original, unedited manuscript directly from the author. It is her vision in its purest form.

Published by Sourcebooks Jabberwocky, an imprint of Sourcebooks, Inc.
P.O. Box 4410, Naperville, Illinois 60567-4410
(630) 961-3900
Fax: (630) 961-2168
www.sourcebooks.com

Cataloging in Publication data is on file with the publisher.

Printed and bound in the United States of America.
IN 10 9 8 7 6 5 4 3 2 1

To Mom,
for simple things

MEET THE

Spiderwort

NAME:
Jensen Fortini

FAIRY NAME AND SPIRIT:
Spiderwort

WAND:
Small, Brilliant Red Cardinal Feather

GIFT:
Cleverness; the ability to come up with good ideas and plans

MENTOR:
Godmother, Madam Chameleon

Periwinkle

NAME:
Vinca Simpson

FAIRY NAME AND SPIRIT:
Periwinkle

WAND:
Elephant's Eyelash

GIFT:
Ability to channel energy from the sun, resistant to heat

MENTOR:
Mrs. Welles, Madam Rose

FAIRY TEAM

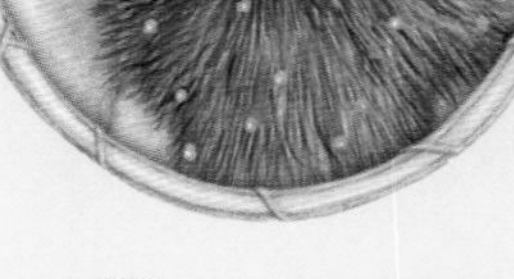

Rosemary

NAME:
Bailey Richardson

FAIRY NAME AND SPIRIT:
Rosemary

WAND:
Nine Strands of Orangutan Hair, Triple Braided

GIFT:
An amazing memory

MENTOR:
Mrs. Clark, Madam Chameleon

Cinnabar

NAME:
Helen Michaels

FAIRY NAME AND SPIRIT:
Cinnabar

WAND:
An Aspen Twig

GIFT:
Enhanced abilities at night

MENTOR:
Mrs. Thompson, Madam Finch

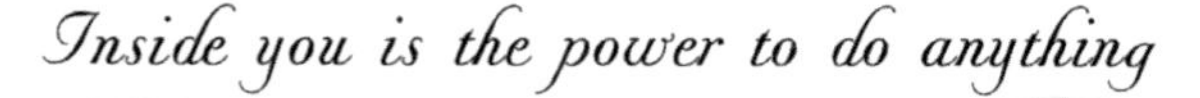

Marigold and the Feather of Hope, the Journey Begins

Dragonfly and the Web of Dreams

Thistle and the Shell of Laughter

Firefly and the Quest of the Black Squirrel

Spiderwort and the Princess of Haiku

Periwinkle and the Cave of Courage

Cinnabar and the Island of Shadows

Mimosa and the River of Wisdom

Come visit us at fairychronicles.com

Contents

Chapter One

The First Day of Summer Vacation

The first day of summer break, what a relief, thought Jensen Fortini, *two whole months of fun*. Jensen had spent the last few weeks working hard in school and looking forward to a relaxing summer vacation. She wouldn't be just lazing around though. In fact, Jensen was one of the busiest girls on the planet because she was also a fairy. This meant that in addition to being just like other nine-year-old girls, Jensen also had a fairy spirit.

Fairies were given the job of protecting nature and fixing problems, mainly problems caused by other magical creatures. This kept Jensen and her fairy friends extremely busy all year long, but it was especially nice to have more time for fairy activities during the summer.

Jensen's fairy spirit came from the spiderwort plant, which was considered to be both a wildflower and an herb, and she was called Spiderwort by other fairies.

Standard fairy form was six inches high. In fairy form, Spiderwort wore a beautiful dress of long, dark green, pointed leaves that came to just above her knees. Brilliant blue flowers with spindly yellow centers were scattered over the bodice and skirt of the dress. Spiderwort also had tall, bright blue wings and wore a headband made of tiny spiderwort flowers to pull back her wavy, strawberry blond hair.

Fairy wands could be made from almost any object and were enchanted to help fairies perform magic. Spiderwort's wand was a small, brilliant red cardinal feather.

She carried the feather in the belt of her fairy dress, along with a small pouch of magic pixie dust and her fairy handbook.

Spiderwort's fairy mentor was her godmother, an older fairy named Madam Chameleon. She was also Spiderwort's mother's best friend, and when not around other fairies, Spiderwort usually called her Aunt Kathy. Madam Chameleon had grown up with Spiderwort's mother and owned a local vegetarian health food restaurant. She also drove a lilac purple Volkswagen Beetle that was a lot of fun to ride in.

In fairy form, Madam Chameleon wore a silvery, greenish-blue dress of a gauzy material that looked like breezy rain. The dress fell almost to her ankles, and she had tiny silver wings. Her wand was a small, straight sprig of mistletoe with a yellowish-green stem and leaves, and pearly white berries.

Madam Chameleon was also mentor to Spiderwort's neighbor and best friend, Bailey Richardson, a rosemary fairy. So far, Spiderwort and Rosemary were the only two herb fairies in the Southwest region of fairies.

As a fairy, Rosemary wore a frosty green dress made of spiky rosemary leaves that were not much like leaves at all, but rather like short thick pine needles. She had blue flowers like Spiderwort, but hers were a very pale creamy blue. And her small wings were a soft, misty green color. Rosemary had shoulder length, light brown hair; and her wand was made of nine strands of orangutan hair, triple braided. She was also the most fragrant of all the fairies and smelled like a mixture of woodsy pine trees and mint.

Rosemary would be coming over to Spiderwort's to play later, after she finished cleaning her room. It was a summertime rule at the Richardsons' house that bedrooms had to be cleaned twice a week. During the school year, Rosemary only had to clean her room once a week; but in the summer, she had more free time and the room tended to get messier.

Spiderwort and Rosemary were planning to skate together and play word games. Both girls loved word games including crossword puzzles, cryptograms, word finds, and anagrams. This afternoon, they were planning to play the Cliché Game. This was a game their teacher at school had made up to help them learn better writing skills. First, they brainstormed a long list of common phrases such as *like two peas in a pod, birds of a feather flock together,* and *things are bigger in Texas*. Next, they formed new statements by mixing up some of the phrases to form different ones like *things are bigger in a pod* and *birds of a feather flock in Texas.* Then they wrote a story using the new sentences they had constructed. Their teacher wanted them to be creative and original, and not write with a lot of overused sayings.

Each fairy was given a special gift relating to her fairy spirit. Spiderwort's gift was cleverness and the ability to come up with good ideas and plans. She was very intuitive and a terrific problem solver. This was one of the reasons she was so good at word puzzles. And she could think her way out of problems more quickly than most girls her age. Spiderwort was also a good chess player and was starting to study debate. She already had the ability to look at all sides of a problem before choosing the best solution.

Rosemary was given an amazing memory as her special fairy gift. Her memorization skills were fantastic. She rarely needed to read things twice and could frequently recite long passages from books after only one reading. This was a tremendous asset to her in school. Because of her ability to remember, Rosemary didn't need to study as many hours as other students, so she achieved good grades with less time and effort.

For *her* fairy gift, Madam Chameleon was given the ability to change colors and blend in with her environment in order to hide. These camouflage skills helped tremendously in performing many fairy functions. Of course, if regular people were to see fairies, they would not be able to recognize them. They would only be able to see the fairy spirits. Spiderwort's mother had seen her daughter, Madam Chameleon, and Rosemary in fairy form several times in the back yard; but to Mrs. Fortini, the fairies only appeared to look like a leafy spiderwort flower, a chameleon lizard, and a rosemary plant. For Madam Chameleon, the ability to blend into her background was very useful in deterring children from chasing her or trying to pick her up.

Non-magical people couldn't see gnomes either because of gnome disguise magic. This was a great benefit to Mr. Tibbons who helped tend the Fortinis' garden as part of his weekly garden route. Mr. Tibbons usually disguised himself as a watermelon, a galvanized bucket, a football, or a rolled up garden hose at the Fortinis' house. These were things that didn't look out of the ordinary in this particular yard and garden. Being magically disguised allowed Mr. Tibbons to go about his business undisturbed and complete his work safely and efficiently.

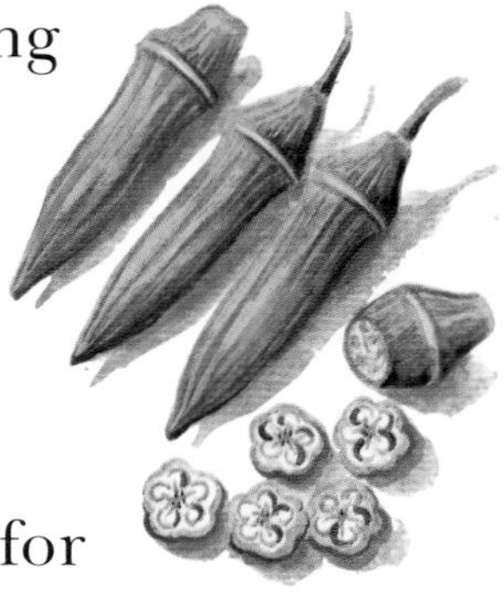

However, fairies could see gnomes as gnomes. Spiderwort had spent an hour early in the morning helping Mr. Tibbons harvest okra and jicama. For the okra, they wore gloves because the okra plants were sticky and itchy. But for the jicama, they just dug in the earth and got their hands good and dirty. Spiderwort's mother was going to make pickled okra later in the week. And she peeled and sliced the jicama to use in salads because the root vegetable was very crunchy and tasty.

Mr. Tibbons was particularly happy today and whistled while he worked. Like all garden gnomes, he was about ten inches high and a dusty brown color all over. He wore overalls with fifteen pockets and rolled-up pant cuffs. In his pockets and pant cuffs, he kept things like roots, seeds, tools, and his yellow bandana. Every so often, he paused in his work to pull out his bandana and wipe his sweaty face.

Mr. Tibbons also chewed on the ends of his long moustache while he worked. Garden gnomes didn't have beards like wood gnomes, but they did have thick bushy moustaches. Periodically, Mr. Tibbons would realize that he was chewing his moustache ends and would blow them out of his mouth with a loud, wet, blubbering whistle.

Spiderwort's calico cat, Pernilla, liked to watch Mr. Tibbons work. They got along very well. In fact, most animals and birds got along well with both gnomes and fairies. Pernilla even helped Mr. Tibbons dig holes sometimes. She liked getting nice and dirty so she could muck up the floors in the house with dusty paw prints. This gave her humans something to do, cleaning up after her artistry, and paying her some extra attention with a little scolding and worrying.

Even though Mr. Tibbons' pockets and pant cuffs were stuffed full of seeds, nuts, and bulbs, he used concentrated gnome magic (and tricks of the gnome trade) to multiply these things so that one seed was usually enough to plant an entire row of radishes or several hills of cucumbers.

Gnomes were given the job of helping plants grow and adding colors to nature. Mr. Tibbons was very well respected in the

gnome community for his colorization techniques, especially with flowers. Today, however, he was coloring bell peppers—red, gold, and green.

After she picked okra, dug jicama, and watched the bell pepper colorization, Spiderwort ran around the house to the backyard compost pile. She turned the heap with a long stick and a small shovel. She was not allowed to use the pitchfork that her father sometimes used to turn the pile because she was too young. The pitchfork was too sharp and not the right size for her, so it could be dangerous. Spiderwort liked spending time outside, and the garden was a good excuse to get away from her sometimes annoying, six-year-old brother, Henry.

When Spiderwort came around the house from the back yard, she noticed the familiar lilac Beetle parked out front. Madam Chameleon was in the living room with Spiderwort's mother. They were in deep discussion, arranging a sleepover at Madam Chameleon's house. Spiderwort kept quiet and let her godmother take care of things without asking any questions. Madam Chameleon was a master of arranging time away from home to participate in fairy activities for both Spiderwort and Rosemary, and her unexpected arrival almost certainly meant they were going to attend a Fairy Circle.

Chapter Two

Emergency Fairy Circle

Fairy Circles were what fairies called their gatherings. Fairies needed to meet regularly to discuss problems and ways to fix them, and to have fairy celebrations.

Sure enough, after Madam Chameleon had explained everything to Spiderwort's mother, the fairy mentor followed Spiderwort to her bedroom to help her pack an overnight bag. In whispers, Madam Chameleon told Spiderwort that they were all going to an emergency Fairy Circle and that she had already arranged with Rosemary's mom for a two-night sleepover.

Rosemary was waiting with her bag by Madam Chameleon's car. She had spent the morning cleaning her room, sweeping up spilled dirt from a potted plant, and remedying a prank played by brownies.

Rosemary had two brownies living in her house. Brownies were boy fairies, about seven inches high. They liked to live in people's houses, and even helped with chores sometimes, but they also liked to play tricks and make messes.

Early in the morning, Brownie Ryan and Brownie Edgar had had a dirt fight in a potted plant. They also removed, and hid, the caps from almost everything in the bathroom including the toothpaste, shaving cream, deodorant, shampoo, conditioner, and mouthwash. So Rosemary had to find the hidden lids and tops, and recap everything. Brownies could be very helpful, but for some reason, Ryan and Edgar were extra mischievous today.

Brownies really liked pastries and milk. So before leaving, Rosemary made sure to put out a jelly donut and some milk for Edgar and Ryan. She hoped this would keep them satisfied, and that they would cool it with the tricks while she was gone. After the cap prank and the potted plant mess, surely they had gotten most of the mischief out of their systems for a while. Rosemary also encouraged the boys to get out of the house for a couple of days to go on an outing or visit other brownies.

Since brownies couldn't fly, they traveled on birds and animals to take trips and carry out important brownie business. A local family of rabbits and two ravens usually took Ryan and Edgar places they needed to go.

Rosemary hoped the brownies would take her suggestion to go away for a couple of days. She didn't want her parents getting frustrated by pranks and messes while she was gone. A certain amount of brownie mischief was fine when she was home because she could help clean up after them and fix things. But Mr. and Mrs. Richardson didn't know they had brownies living in the house. If they found out, Ryan and Edgar would probably get thrown out.

As they piled into her car, Madam Chameleon told Spiderwort and Rosemary, "I got a nut message from Madam Toad. It must be something pretty important to call a meeting on such short notice."

(Nut messages were hollowed-out nuts with notes and letters secreted inside. Birds and animals liked to deliver them for the fairies.)

"We're going to pick up Periwinkle on the way," added Madam Chameleon. "Madam Rose arranged for her to have a sleepover with us."

Periwinkle's name was Vinca Simpson. When they picked her up, and crowded her bag into the already cramped purple Beetle, Periwinkle was bubbling with excitement. This was probably going to be the best summer of her life because her foster family was legally adopting her. Mr. and

Mrs. Martinez were the third foster family Periwinkle had lived with since her parents died when she was five. They already had a ten-year-old daughter named Megan.

Periwinkle usually got along well with her new sister. However, just this week there had been some friction over Periwinkle being allowed to begin taking pottery classes this fall, and Megan having to wait until next year to start piano lessons. Periwinkle wanted to take pottery classes very badly. She was of Native American descent and wanted to learn a craft that was part of her heritage.

Periwinkle was feeling guilty about the pottery classes because she knew that her adoption had cost money, and this was probably why Megan would have to wait for piano lessons. She also knew that her new parents were anxious to make her feel welcome into the family, and this might be why she was going to be able to take lessons first. Periwinkle had told her parents that the only thing that was important to her was to have a real family again, this time for the rest of her life, and that she didn't need presents or other gifts. But her parents had made the decision, and Megan was disappointed.

As a fairy, Periwinkle wore a rosy pink, flower petal dress. Her pale pink wings were very tiny and feathery, and she wore a periwinkle flower hairclip to hold back her long dark hair. Periwinkle's wand was one of the most unique in the fairy realm—an elephant's eyelash. The eyelash was dark gray, long, and slightly curved.

For her special fairy gift, Periwinkle was given the ability to channel energy from the sun. She also had great tolerance to heat and sun, just like pink periwinkle flowers in nature. In addition to her special gift, Periwinkle's Native American heritage gave her extra abilities in the wilderness. She could identify plants that could be eaten safely, recognize various animal tracks, and tell directions without a compass.

Periwinkle was also the only fairy with a spirit guide. He took the form of a small snail and rode on her shoulder, giving her guidance and advice when needed.

Talking about their plans for the summer and boys at school, the girls chatted for some time while Madam Chameleon drove.

Madam Toad always chose the sites for Fairy Circles very carefully. They usually met under trees with special meaning. As Madam Chameleon parked the car on the side of a country road near a densely wooded area, she told the girls, "We are meeting under a hazel tree this time. This means our discussion will have something to do with poetry, meditation, or inspiration." The fairies were very excited; they had never met under a hazel tree before.

As they entered the group of fairies, Spiderwort pulled her friend Dragonfly aside to have a word with her about two brochures they were collaborating on. Fairies were very concerned about recycling and conservation, and Spiderwort and Dragonfly were working on some writing projects together. Currently, they were brainstorming ideas for two informational leaflets. The first was called *21 Further Uses for Soda Bottles*, and the second was titled *The Next Great Adventure for Steel Cans—36 Practical Ideas for Home and Office*. It was a good idea to reuse items whenever possible. The girls hoped to finish these brochures over the summer and get them printed up to distribute at school in the fall.

After she had exchanged several ideas with Dragonfly, Spiderwort caught up with Rosemary and Periwinkle to say hello to Lily, Snapdragon, Tulip, Pumpkinwing, Morning Glory, Primrose, and Hollyhock.

Before nearly every meeting, the fairies had refreshments and got a chance to visit with friends. They enjoyed their usual fairy fare of powdered sugar puff pastries, raspberries, lemon jellybeans, peanut butter and marshmallow crème sandwiches, and homemade fudge. But today they also had special treats of homemade bread-and-butter pickles that Dragonfly's mom had made in a crock, and home-canned yummy peach butter on tiny biscuits baked by Madam Swallowtail.

Primrose was staying close to her cousin, Hollyhock, in order to interpret for her if needed. Hollyhock was the only deaf fairy in their group, but she could read lips very well and usually only needed an interpreter if a speaker was too far away to see the mouth clearly. Many of the fairies were taking American Sign Language classes. And at each Fairy Circle, they were learning a little sign language. The group had already learned the alphabet, so all of the fairies could fingerspell. Now they were starting to learn words and some whole sentences.

Two new fairies joined Fairy Circle today, a cinnabar moth fairy and a mimosa fairy.

Cinnabar's name was Helen Michaels. She was a thin, willowy black girl with

Cinnabar

straight dark hair that came just to her shoulders. As a fairy, Cinnabar wore a dress made of black velvet fuzz, and she had large, brilliant red wings with sooty gray striping along the tips. She was very graceful and was taking ballet classes. Cinnabar carried a small aspen twig for her wand, and her special fairy gift involved the ability to function well at night. She had more energy and could fly better and see better at night. Cinnabar was somewhat shy and reserved, but all of the other fairies were drawn to her because of her grace and beauty.

The mimosa fairy had long blond hair. Her name was Alexandra Hastings, and she wore a dress made of silky, glistening, mimosa flower strands in soft colors of peach, light pink, white, and dark pink. Mimosa had tall, peach colored wings and smelled like fresh ripe peaches. She carried a curly emu feather wand. As her special fairy gift, Mimosa was blessed with sensitivity, caring, and intuitiveness that included the ability to give counsel and comfort to others.

Spiderwort, Rosemary, and Periwinkle were all mesmerized by the new additions to their group. Between Cinnabar and Mimosa, they couldn't decide who was the most beautiful. But they definitely thought these were the most beautiful fairies of all time. Of course, last year, they had felt this way about Starfish and Milkweed when they first met them. The truth was that all fairies were beautiful, even Madam Toad. It was just the newness that made Cinnabar and Mimosa so attractive, like new dolls or toys that seem better than the old ones for a short time.

The day was beautiful. Sunlight streamed sideways through the low-hanging branches of the hazel tree, creating a lacy pattern of shadows on the grassy ground.

Madam Toad soon called the meeting to order, and Primrose taught everyone several new words from American Sign Language. They learned the signs for friends, family, summer, butterfly, home, eat, walk, swim, beautiful, rainbow, clouds, please, and sorry.

Next, Madam Toad began to explain the reason for their emergency meeting. "Before we begin, I want you to look up something in your handbooks. Look up Princess of Haiku," she instructed.

The fairies all flipped the pages of their handbooks to find the Princess of Haiku:

> *Princess of Haiku: The Princess of Haiku is the Spirit of Simplicity and the source of all simple pleasure on earth. To some, she is known as the Lyrist of Inner Peace and Modest Desires. The princess draws inspiration from simple haiku poems, and spreads the ability to take pleasure from simple things to all of*

mankind. She is very old, possibly as old as many of the elves—the oldest known magical creatures. Her only enemies are two evil spirits: the Phantom of Excess and the Specter of Pandemonium. Currently, these evil spirits occupy two ogres, twin sisters named Chaotica Glut and Plethora Glut. Over the years, the spirits have pursued the Princess of Haiku. However, as long as simple pleasure exists on earth, the princess is strong and they cannot touch her.

When the fairies finished reading, Madam Toad continued. "The Princess of Haiku is missing. I have consulted Mother Nature. We are not sure if she has been kidnapped, or if she is just lost. And at this point, we don't know if the Glut sisters are involved.

"Already, it is obvious that something is very wrong. The princess is not just on an unexplained holiday. Simple pleasure is already being affected. If we don't find her, and help to correct the problem, simple pleasure will disappear completely."

As the fairies listened carefully, Madam Toad explained further. "Dissatisfaction in simple things is growing. It has started in children and will soon spread to adults. Eventually, this problem will affect all other creatures as well. If the situation is not corrected, all pleasure in simple things will be lost to greed, chaos, and materialism."

Next, Madam Toad announced which fairies would be participating in the fairy adventure. "I have decided that Spiderwort will lead this mission. We have little to go on, and Spiderwort is a quick thinker with excellent problem-solving skills. Rosemary, Periwinkle, and Cinnabar will accompany her; and Madam Chameleon will supervise. In this group, we have a very diverse set of fairy gifts and strengths. Hopefully, the team will be able to find the Princess of Haiku and fix what is wrong.

"I can hardly tell you where to begin," Madam Toad added. "However, I have consulted that oak tree over there and have obtained a riddle." The fairies all looked toward where Madam Toad had pointed and saw a massive live oak tree on a hill in the distance.

Oak trees were very wise and could see the future. But they didn't give up their wisdom easily. In fact, they didn't like to give advice at all because they were afraid of changing the future. However, they did sometimes offer riddles in the hopes that people would give up before solving them. And if someone did happen to solve a difficult riddle, the oak tree was still satisfied because, obviously, the outcome was meant to be.

"Here is the riddle," Madam Toad said. "'*The beginning lies in the center of the field that only smart birds may enter.*'"

The fairies thought for a while. Then

The beginning
lies in the
center of
the field
that only
smart birds
may ent

Madam Toad added, "Aside from the riddle, I can offer you this advice. I believe the path will be marked by simplicity. Seek out things that are plain, bleak, unadorned, and stark. If you are presented with choices, try to take the simple path, the one that has not been traveled. Choose things that are uncomplicated—things that lead to simplicity." After a short pause, the fairy leader finished with, "This is all I can tell you. Good luck. I am confident that you will be able figure this out."

Backpacks had already been readied for each member of the group and included blankets, pillows, food, and water. The packs were chock full of peanut butter and marshmallow crème sandwiches, lemon jellybeans, raspberries, and powdered sugar puff pastries. There were enough provisions to last several days if needed.

Chapter Three

The Scarecrow

As most of the fairies left, Spiderwort sat thinking. After a few minutes, she said, "I have an idea; follow me." She led as Rosemary, Periwinkle, Cinnabar, and Madam Chameleon followed. The group flew out of the woods and into an area of open farmland.

While the fairies traveled, they visited with Cinnabar to get to know her better. She attended a different elementary school, and the other girls were anxious to learn more about her. Cinnabar was somewhat quiet, but she did answer questions about her family and hobbies. She also told her new friends

the Scarecrow

about the ballet classes she had been taking for nearly four years.

Flying low to the ground, the fairies only made one detour when Periwinkle warned them about a patch of nettles. The group carefully avoided the itchy, stinging plants and flew on.

After about an hour, Spiderwort landed on a cedar fencepost and said, "I think this is where we need to be." She had stopped at the edge of a large cornfield. The corn was a beautiful, rippling green and was about three feet high. In the center of the field stood a large scarecrow.

Spiderwort smiled as she told her friends, "This is certainly a field that only smart birds, those not fooled by scarecrows, may enter. I hope this is the answer to the riddle. Before we fly out there though," she added, "I want to check something in my handbook."

As the others waited, Spiderwort looked up scarecrows:

"Scarecrows: Gardeners and farmers use scarecrows to frighten birds and animals away from plants and crops. Scarecrows are not usually very frightening in appearance, but the movement of their clothes in the breeze may scare away some animals and birds. However, over the years, scarecrows have not been very effective and are now used mainly for decoration in many parts of the country. It is more advisable to tie tin pie plates from trees or posts. The noise and movement of the pie plates in the wind have a much greater ability to frighten away birds than billowing scarecrow clothes. Many animals have gotten used to people, and are smart enough that human figures do not scare them. Scarecrow is also a term used to describe

anything that is frightening or scary, but not actually dangerous."

After reading the entry aloud, Spiderwort told her companions, "I thought the handbook might have some advice for us, or some information about scarecrows that we didn't know."

As she looked back down at the pages of her handbook, she was startled to see an entry addressed directly to her:

Spiderwort (Jensen),

This scarecrow is special. Talk to him. He can tell you something about the Princess of Haiku.

The group of fairies approached the scarecrow somewhat apprehensively. None of them had ever talked to a scarecrow before. He was dressed in yellow overalls with a red shirt underneath, and he wore blue tennis shoes. His hat was wide brimmed, made of straw, and decorated with a blue band.

Spiderwort took the lead and addressed him. "Hello, Mr. Scarecrow. We are fairies on a special mission. I am Spiderwort and this is Periwinkle, Rosemary, Cinnabar, and Madam Chameleon. We were wondering if you might be able to help us."

The scarecrow turned his head a little to one side, smiled, and replied, "Hello, fairies. It is a very fine day in this cornfield and, yes, I think I can help you and I need your help too."

He paused and turned his head to the other side before going on. "I have been here for two days, hoping you would come by. If I am not mistaken, you are seeking the Princess of Haiku. She is a very good friend of mine. We have been long-time companions. I can take you on the path to her location, but you must do the work to find her."

As he finished speaking, the scarecrow jumped down from his wooden perch;

then he reached behind a row of corn to lift another scarecrow out of hiding. He placed the substitute on the perch he had just vacated, and explained, "I borrowed his perch while I waited for you."

The fairies flew as the scarecrow walked. He led them through two more sown fields—one with oats and one with soybeans. As they traveled, the scarecrow told the fairies that the princess would tell them her story when they arrived. However, he warned them that the princess was guarded by two ogres.

To get more information, Spiderwort looked up ogres in her handbook and read aloud to her friends:

> "*Ogres: Ogres are large magical creatures, generally fifteen to twenty feet tall, which is about half the size of giants. They are very mean and scary, and should be*

considered dangerous, especially because some creatures believe that ogres like to eat human beings. However, since they are so large, ogres usually do not concern themselves with things as small as fairies. Ogres are quick to anger, but they are not very bright and can be easily tricked or confused."

Finally, the group came to the edge of a small forest.

"This is the first test of the journey," the scarecrow said.

On the ground, in front of two tall pine trees, sat a beautiful sparkling ruby as large as a golf ball. Next to the ruby sat a tiny, smooth gray river stone about the size of pea.

"You must choose the correct one and take it with you on the journey," the scarecrow instructed. "But you only have one choice, so make it a good one."

"This is easy so far," said Spiderwort, immediately picking up the river stone and slipping it into her pocket.

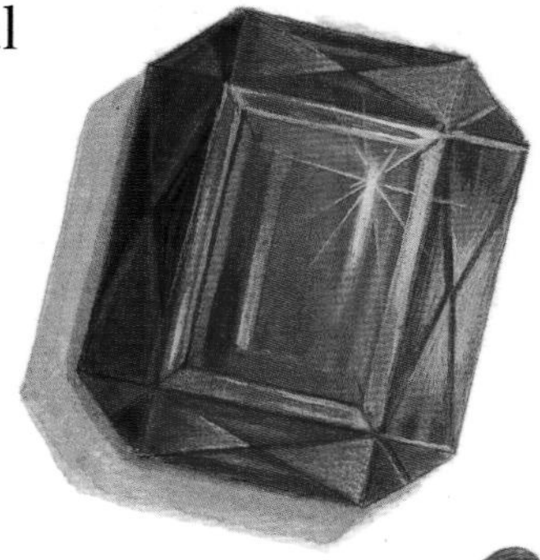

As she did this, several low-hanging boughs of the two pine trees parted and revealed a path through the forest.

"Good, good!" said the scarecrow. "You obviously know exactly what you are seeking."

The group traveled a short way down the path and came to a small door in a tree trunk. About four feet high, the shiny brass door had a large keyhole and a tiny glass doorknob. Next to the tree trunk sat a stone table full of keys. There were about twenty-five keys in all, made of various kinds of metal, intricately wrought and very ornate. Most of the keys were made of iron, silver, or pewter. Three gold keys were the exception to this.

"Again, you can choose only one," said

the scarecrow, "and you only have one choice, so choose wisely."

The collection seemed an overwhelming assortment for such an important decision. Spiderwort and the others looked at the keys carefully. None of them were plain; none of them were simple.

"There must be some clue here," said Spiderwort. "Which type of metal is most simple?"

Her friends didn't know.

Spiderwort continued to look over the embellished keys with the hope that the right one would magically jump out at her. *This is way too complex*, she thought. Then she said, "The simplest thing would be if the door were already unlocked."

On impulse, she grasped the tiny glass doorknob with both hands and turned. To her delight, and the surprise of everyone, the door immediately swung open. It had indeed been unlocked.

"Excellent!" cried the scarecrow. "All of the keys fit the lock, but they have a spell on them. They are locking keys only, not unlocking keys. If you had tried any of the keys, the door would have been permanently locked."

On another impulse, Spiderwort raised her cardinal feather wand and took a handful of pixie dust out of the little pouch on her belt. Sprinkling the glittering dust over the table of keys, she pointed her wand and uttered, "*Disappear*." A small stream of blue light issued from the tip of her wand, and the keys all vanished. "So if anyone needs to follow us," she explained, "they can."

The scarecrow nodded approvingly. "A fairy of action," he said, admiringly. "I'm impressed."

As they passed through the door (the scarecrow stooping to make it through), they entered a dark clearing.

The fairies all whispered, "*Fairy light*," and the tips of their wands glowed brightly to light the area. On the far side of the clearing, three paths led off through the trees.

"Another choice, and again, only one," the scarecrow instructed.

The first path was snowy, and the snow was marred with very large deep footprints, as though someone had recently traveled the trail. The second was a dusty path with an obvious line of red berries scattered and dropped along the trail, as if luring someone to follow. The third path was made of sparkling sand disappearing through the trees. The sand was completely smooth and undisturbed; and the golden smoothness glittered with purple and green particles, reflecting the light from the fairies' wands.

As Spiderwort thought about the choices, the others gave input to help her decide.

Periwinkle's spirit guide advised her to say, "The snowy path looks as though ogres have recently passed through. They have left footprints for us to follow."

Rosemary countered with her own idea. "But the dusty path has a line of berries. That is just what I would do, if I were the princess and wanted someone to follow my trail to help me."

Spiderwort thought over the possibilities before telling them of her choice.

"The snowy path is stark," she told her friends. "And the dusty path is bleak, except for the berries. But I think the correct choice is the sandy path. Even though the sand glitters with the reflection of our light, the trail has not been traveled. Remember what Madam Toad told us about choosing the least traveled path."

"Good choice," said Madam Chameleon. "I believe you are correct." Spiderwort blushed a little at the praise of her mentor.

No one questioned her decision, but followed her confidently down the sandy path, before the scarecrow even had a chance to confirm that she had made the right choice, which he did several moments later. "You are making very good decisions," he said. "Perhaps you *can* help the princess. There is only one more hurdle to overcome to reach her."

As he said this, they came to what looked like two curtains hanging from curtain rods on invisible windows. In fact, the curtain rods seemed to be hanging by themselves, in midair. One of the curtains was white, and the other was black.

"This is a tough choice," said Spiderwort, for again, just like the problem with the keys, she could find no clues. Thinking aloud, she said, "The only difference between the curtains is the color. I remember learning about the color wheel in my art class. Black is every color mixed together,

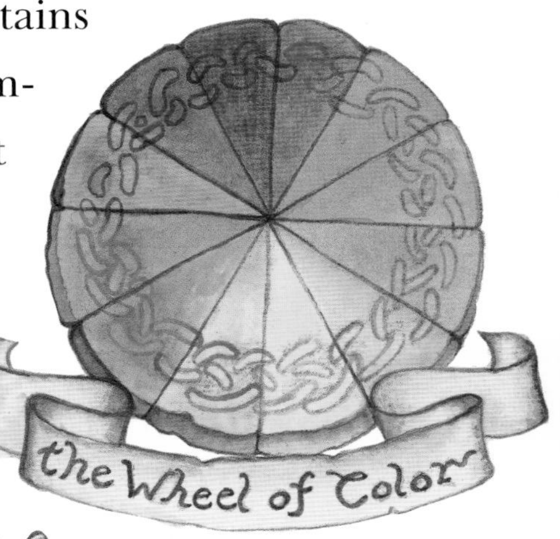

sort of like a rainbow made of midnight; and white is the absence of color. So black is very complex, and white is simpler. My choice is the white curtain."

The scarecrow smiled and nodded. Again, the clever fairy had made a wise choice.

Next, Spiderwort pulled open the white curtain, and the group of travelers passed through the opening she revealed. In a large forest clearing, floating in what seemed to be a giant egg of light, sat the tiny Princess of Haiku.

Chapter Four

The Princess's Story

The Princess of Haiku may have been old, but she looked like a child, not much older than seven or eight. She was petite, with fair skin and jet-black hair pulled into two tiny pigtails above her ears. She was dressed in a red shirt with yellow sleeves. She also wore blue pants and sneakers.

"Of course," said Spiderwort, "the primary colors on the color wheel—red, blue, and yellow. What could be simpler?" Then she added, "You are the Princess of Haiku."

"Yes," the princess said, nodding. "I have been hoping someone would come, but I hardly dared to hope that anyone could help."

The Princess of Haiku

is the Spirit of Simplicity & the source of all simple pleasure on Earth. To some she is known as the Lyrist of Inner Peace and Modest Desires.

Directly behind the hovering and glowing egg of light were the two ogres. They were very large, at about fifteen feet high, with giant feet and hands. The ogres had untidy, bushy brown hair sticking out in all directions. Both of the sisters Glut wore ugly, mustard-colored dresses that were torn and hung in rags unevenly about their legs. When they noticed the fairies, the ogres jumped up angrily and stomped their feet. The ground shook.

The Princess of Haiku acted quickly and called to the sisters. "They are just here to say goodbye to me. Don't worry!"

This seemed to satisfy the ogres because they grinned evilly and returned to what they were doing, which was kneeling facing each other over a hole dug in the ground. Several coconuts surrounded the hole. Chaotica and Plethora Glut were playing with the coconuts, rolling them around and trying to knock the other coconuts out of the way while aiming for the hole.

The princess told the fairies, "I taught them how to play marbles, with coconuts so they would be the right size. They are really enjoying themselves."

"How can you be nice to them when they are keeping you prisoner?" asked Spiderwort.

"The Glut sisters don't really mean me any harm," the princess answered. "The spirits possessing them are much more dangerous. However, since the ogres are having fun, enjoying the simple pleasure of playing marbles, it's rather like a battle of wills. The Specter of Pandemonium and the Phantom of Excess are pretty upset right now because they don't have complete control over the ogres.

"Chaotica and Plethora have their own wills," the princess continued, "even though they are possessed by evil spirits. Ogres are easily tricked and confused, but try getting them to stop doing something they enjoy.

It would take about twelve tons of bricks to get them to stop. The specter and phantom don't have that kind of power. The ogres won't harm you as long as you don't try to free me from the egg. They are just watching over me until I vanish."

As the fairies looked at one another in confusion, the princess explained, "I am under a *Spell of Diminishment*. The specter and phantom did not cause this, and neither did the ogres. But before I tell you my story, I need you to do something." The princess pointed across the clearing as she told the fairies, "Go to the pond over there and toss in the small river pebble that you brought with you."

The scarecrow sat cross-legged on the ground next to the hovering princess while the fairies did as she requested. They noticed that the princess seemed to fade out a little as they were heading off to the pond, almost as though she were disappearing. However, a second later she was visible again, strong and clear.

The fairies flew to the edge of the small pond and watched closely as Spiderwort took the little stone from her pocket and tossed it into the center of the water. There was a tiny splash and a small slurp. Then, ripples from the center, where the stone had entered, began to make their way outward toward the edges of the water. It took several minutes for the surface of the water to become completely calm and smooth again.

When the fairies returned to the princess, they were surprised to discover that a ghost had joined her, floating next to the egg of light. He was a milky-silver color all over and was dressed in flowing robes.

"This is my friend, the bard," said the princess. "You will get a chance to hear his story after I tell you mine." Then she asked, "Do you understand what you have just seen in the pond?"

"I think so," said Spiderwort. "One single event has occurred and has resulted in a ripple effect. Even though what happened first was small, it caused a chain reaction and is spreading to much larger consequences."

"Very good," responded the princess. "Now let me tell you what has happened. For many years, I have been fading. Most people are no longer content with small pleasures. Children do not enjoy simple games as much as they used to. Few are satisfied with playing cat's cradle, blowing bubbles, flying kites, building sand castles, drawing sidewalk chalk pictures, or making mud pies. They tend to like video games and highly technical, motorized toys such as radio-controlled cars and planes."

Cinnabar looked down and shifted a little nervously. She very much enjoyed playing video games.

The princess went on with her story. "Also, some children are not satisfied with just three or four video games; they feel they must have thirty or forty, or more. Many children would also rather play on a computer than read a book or do a crossword puzzle. This is not limited to children, of course. There is also a growing desire to acquire more than what is actually needed for happiness and fulfillment. I know of a family of four that has five computers; and there is another family of three with six telephones: one for each of them inside the house, and three more to take with them when they go out.

"Many people also do not appreciate simple things even when stared in the face with them—things like falling leaves and singing birds. For people with complex desires, it is almost impossible for them to take pleasure in something like observing the changing colors of a chameleon lizard, seeing a beautiful red moth, smelling a rosemary bush, or glimpsing a tiny snail."

As the princess said this, she looked directly at Periwinkle whose eyes widened in surprise. Usually, no one but Periwinkle could see her spirit guide sitting on her shoulder. The princess paused a moment longer before continuing her story.

"However, as long as one person on earth takes pleasure in simple things, I can still exist, even in a faded state. But this brings me to why I am under a *Spell of Diminishment*, and what will happen if the spell is not broken." The Princess of Haiku sighed deeply as she went on. "A young child recently had a birthday. Her parents were very poor and were unable to buy many gifts for her. Her mother baked a cake, and they were able to buy her a jumprope and a book of poetry. She wanted a computer, several dolls, and a lot of new clothes. The little girl was so upset not to have received the gifts she desired that she threw away the jumprope. Then she tore up the book of poetry and threw it away as well.

"Her parents were heartbroken that they couldn't afford nicer things for her, and that they were not able to please her on her birthday. Of course they wanted to give her nice things, every parent wants this for their child, but they also had to be able to purchase food and pay the electric bill.

"What the little girl didn't know is that books of poetry contain a spell. If they are destroyed before they are read by at least one person, the spell is released. It is a *Spell of Diminishment* directed at me. I will diminish and vanish within a few days if the spell is not broken.

"But that is not the worst of it," the princess told them. "With my diminishment, a chain effect will occur. The world will gradually lose the ability to experience simple pleasure, and the problem will not stop there. Eventually, greed, materialism, and excess will take over. And soon after, all pleasure will be lost.

"Even massive acquisition will not be enough for the inhabitants of the world. People will no longer be able to be satisfied no matter how many things they have, or how

much fun they experience. There will be pandemonium and chaos, and nothing will ever be enough to fulfill mankind's desires. The world will become hopelessly complex; there will be no joy or peace of mind for anyone."

Spiderwort could contain herself no longer. There was a kind of frantic panic building inside her, and she interrupted the princess. "How do we break the spell?" she asked.

The princess answered, "A child released the spell; only a child can break it."

"We may be fairies, but we are also children," said Spiderwort. "Tell us what to do!"

The princess looked respectfully at Spiderwort, but smiled a little sadly. After a few moments, she said wearily, "Very well, I am hopeful that you can help. The bard will tell you what must be done to break the spell, but you should first hear his story."

Chapter Five

The Bard's Instructions

"Hello," said the bard. "Yes, I can tell you how to break the spell. It is a mighty challenge, but if you are diligent and clever, you may accomplish it.

"First, let me explain who I am. I was the Minstrel of Epic Poetry, and I have been a friend to the Princess of Haiku for many long ages. In fact, we were cousins, created to balance each other. Haiku are short, simple poems, while epics are long, complex poems. I am here now to accompany her into diminishment so she will not have to make the journey alone. Hopefully, you will succeed, and this will not be necessary."

Bard

The bard smiled sadly as he continued. "I diminished many years ago. People were searching for meaning in their lives and decided to simplify somewhat. They stopped writing epic poetry. A few epic poems have been written in recent ages, but none have become classics because there is not the heart and soul poured into them like the poetry of old.

"Without new epic poetry to sustain me, I diminished under another *Spell of Diminishment*. Now, I only exist in shadow, and occasionally in reflection, when someone reads classic epic poetry or tries to write a new epic poem. But I can never come back because that is the nature of total diminishment."

The bard paused for a moment before going on. "There are three parts to breaking the *Spell of Diminishment* to release the princess. The first part involves a list of things you must experience."

"Oh, I don't have anything to write with," said Spiderwort, worriedly.

"Don't worry," said Rosemary. "I can remember lists with no problem." With this, she leaned forward to carefully catch every word of the bard's instructions.

"You must experience the following things:

nature's heartbeat

the whisper of butterfly wings

music in the water

a night halo

the smell of rain

a sunrise

love in a flower, and bring it back

"The last item is the only thing you will need to bring back with you."

As the bard finished reciting the list, Rosemary said confidently, "Got it."

And Spiderwort added, "It's like a scavenger hunt. We are good at things like this."

"Then be off quickly," said the bard. "There are two other tasks you must also complete to break the spell. The scarecrow and I will stay with the princess and keep an eye on the ogres while you are gone."

The ogres were still having fun playing marbles with coconuts, and were completely ignoring the fairies. So the fairies flew quickly into the forest to begin working on their first task.

Chapter Six

Scavenger Hunt

“Too bad Madam Monarch or Madam Swallowtail is not here,” said Periwinkle. “We could have taken care of the whispering butterfly wings right away. I suppose a moth wouldn’t count,” she added, glancing at Cinnabar.

“Probably not,” agreed Spiderwort, as they reached the edge of a small clearing. “We should stick to the list exactly.”

“Nature’s heartbeat is first,” said Rosemary.

As the fairies were thinking about this, two brownies arrived through the trees, riding on a bobcat.

"Hello!" the brownies said in unison, sliding down the bobcat's front legs. The brownies looked so much alike, the fairies decided that they had to be twins. They were right.

"Fairies!" said one of the twins, delightedly. He smiled and introduced himself. "I'm John; this is my brother James. We're twins and we're eleven. Brownie twins also have nicknames," he added. "You can call us either James and John, or Donnybrook and Ruckus."

Both James and John were grinning broadly.

The fairies backed away a little apprehensively at the mention of the nicknames, since the words basically meant the same thing as fighting and stirring up trouble.

Spiderwort introduced herself and each of the other fairies. Then, laughing a little nervously, she asked, "You don't want to wrestle or fight with us, do you? We don't have Thistle with us. She is the only fairy who really knows how to fight."

The boys looked aghast at her question, and James said, "We don't fight with fairies. We like fairies." As he said this, he glanced at Cinnabar and looked down, blushing a little and shuffling his feet as he stuffed his hands into his pockets.

John added, "But we know Thistle; she's our friend. We wouldn't fight with her either. We pretty much only donnybrook and ruckus with other brownies."

Both boys were again grinning at the fairies. James and John were nearly identical, except John seemed to have more freckles. Brownies derived their spirits from earthy

things like mosses, river stones, mushrooms, crystals, and pinecones. James and John were both granite rock brownies and wore strings of polished granite chips around their necks.

The fairies were relieved that the twins were not going to pick a fight, and they explained their mission to the boys. Even though brownies liked to play tricks on fairies, they had worked together with fairies several times before to solve problems.

James told them, "I think we can help you with the first item on your list. How would you like to listen to the heartbeat of a bobcat?" The fairies all looked at each other excitedly, and nodded.

"Be careful though," added James. "He's a little ticklish, and it's not wise to tickle a bobcat."

Lying on his side on the ground, very still, the bobcat let each of the fairies lean onto his chest and listen to his heartbeat. He actually purred a little because it was not unpleasant to have fairies hugging his chest and pressing their tiny ears into his fur. And they were careful not to tickle him, which he appreciated very much.

After each fairy had the chance to hear the fast-thumping heartbeat, they thanked the bobcat and the brownies. The group was just about to leave to seek the next item on their list when another brownie rode into the clearing on a small rabbit.

Brownie Christopher was the leader of the brownies, and the fairies had met him before at Fairy Circle. He was an acorn brownie and was a couple of years older than the twins. He was also much more serious.

"Hello," Christopher greeted them. "I talked to Madam Toad this morning," he added. "She told me to keep a lookout for you. I hope everything is going okay with your mission."

Spiderwort told Christopher of their progress so far, and especially praised

James and John for their help. She hoped that the twins would get *brownie* points from their leader for helping the fairies.

Christopher looked closely at James and John, who had kept quiet in his presence. Then the brownie leader nodded slowly and said, "I hope you will always get help from the brownies whenever you need or ask for it." James and John both shuffled their feet and stuffed their hands into their pockets.

Next, Christopher addressed John. "Bad news, I'm afraid. I need you to take over feather duties for one month. Brownie Marcus has the flu, and the timing is unfortunate."

Brownies were the keepers of the Feather of Hope. This was a tremendous responsibility because the Feather of Hope was the source of all hope on earth. The brownies were tasked with the job of traveling all over the world with the feather to replenish the supply of hope for all creatures inhabiting the earth.

Christopher continued. "The reason you will have to feather-keep for a whole month is that the feather is needed in Australia and New Zealand. We only have to go there once a year, but the time is now. We cannot delay. You will need to travel by gull, whale, and dolphin to get there. Last year, Brownie Alan managed to catch a plane to Australia by traveling with someone's pet cat. But we can't wait around hoping to get lucky with a traveling pet or zoo animal. You must leave today. While you are there, fly as high as you

can. Remember, the higher you fly, the more hope is spread and the longer it lasts."

The fairies noticed that as John listened, his whole attitude changed. He was very serious. His smile had completely disappeared, and he was concentrating intently on Christopher's words.

"There will be plenty of birds and animals to help you," Christopher added. "Emus, pelicans, and kangaroos are usually the most helpful.

"But be careful down there. Remember what happened two years ago with Brownie Joel. A kindly wallaby got used to carrying him around in her pouch and didn't want to let him go. It was more of an emotional struggle than a physical one, but we can't afford those kinds of entanglements."

As he said this, Christopher glanced sharply at James who was scratching behind the bobcat's ears. James stopped scratching immediately when Christopher looked at him. Then the bobcat looked disdainfully at James, hoping for the scratching to begin again.

As the brownie leader noticed the fairies taking an interest in what he was saying, Christopher added, "I could tell you some stories. We had a problem last year in West Texas with Brownie Andrew and a mountain lion. It wasn't that the mountain lion didn't want to let Andrew go. But they got so attached to one another that the mountain lion decided to go everywhere with Andrew, and that was not good. We can't have a mountain lion in back yards, garden sheds, and public parks. I had to give them both a talking to."

Christopher had been carrying the feather in a sling on his back. He lifted the sling over his head and carefully handed it to John, who equally carefully lowered the feather over his own head and placed the sling securely on his shoulder. John immediately climbed onto the bobcat, and with a nod to all of them, set off at once.

For their brief encounter with the Feather of Hope, the fairies had a renewed sense of strong hope that they would be successful in their mission.

James mounted the rabbit with Christopher. Then the brownies waved to the fairies as the rabbit bounded off through the bushes and trees.

Just before they left, James had been standing next to Cinnabar. After the brownies departed, she noticed that he had put several stick-burrs in her hair.

"Oh, what a mean trick!" she said, her eyes suddenly filling with tears as she tried to remove the burrs.

Madam Chameleon turned Cinnabar around to help get the burrs loose. As she did this, she quietly told Cinnabar, "It just means that he likes you, Helen. He didn't bother to play a prank on anyone else."

Cinnabar's tears immediately stopped, and a dark blush crept up her neck and onto her face. In fact, with her red wings and equally red face, she almost looked as though she were on fire.

Madam Chameleon removed the last and most stubborn stick-burr with a little wave of her mistletoe wand while uttering the word, "*Release*." Then, smiling, the fairy mentor added, "If I'm not mistaken, James left you a note in a nut message."

There was a tiny sunflower seed at Cinnabar's feet. She picked it up and discovered that it was indeed a nut message. The sunflower seed had a hinge on one side. Cinnabar opened it and found a note inside from James. She snapped the nut shut almost at once, without sharing it with the other fairies, and hastily put the seed in her pocket. She would read the note later, by herself. The other girls did not ask her about it, but they all smiled.

It had started to drizzle.

"Thank goodness," said Spiderwort. "The smell of rain—one more thing on the list."

Next, the fairies flew across a wide meadow in search of water and butterflies; and they found what they were looking for. At the edge of the meadow, they could see a small lake through the thinning trees. As they neared the water, a large satyr butterfly drifted lazily out of the bushes. The fairies were very excited.

The satyr was dark brown with large, yellow-ringed eyespots on his wings. They flew alongside the butterfly, and he didn't seem to mind. Fairies and butterflies usually got along very well with one another. As they flew together over the water, along with the breeze and the hum of their own fairy wings, they heard the slow, rhythmic whispers of the movement of the satyr's wings. When each of the fairies had heard the whispers and nodded to Spiderwort, they waved goodbye to the butterfly and flew to the edge of the lake.

They sat together on the bank of a small cove. Again, they were in luck. A slow, melodious whistling came from a quiet corner of the cove.

"Music in the water," said Spiderwort happily. The fairies were hearing the sound of evening breezes flowing through reeds growing in the shallows of the lake inlet.

The fairies sat together contentedly, full of hope, and had a wonderful dinner of peanut butter and marshmallow crème sandwiches and raspberries, while they listened to the reeds making music and watched the sun go down.

"There are only three things left," said Rosemary. "A night halo, a sunrise, and love in a flower."

As the sun completely disappeared behind the trees at the far edge of the lake, Cinnabar told the others, "I will search for the halo and return for you. Don't worry about me, I actually work better in the dark." Madam Chameleon nodded her consent for Cinnabar to depart alone, and the moth fairy took off in a slow, graceful arc, disappearing behind them through the trees.

Cinnabar returned less than an hour later.

"I found it," she said breathlessly, beaming happily.

The other fairies followed as she led them back to the meadow they had passed through. As Cinnabar pointed to the sky, the fairies gasped in surprise at what they saw. The moon was nearly full and hung just over the trees at the far end of the meadow. Around the moon was a distinct halo, like a soft ring of golden light.

Spiderwort was thumbing through her fairy handbook.

"It's here!" she exclaimed, excitedly. "There's an entry." In the dim glow of moonlight, she read aloud to them:

> *"Ring Around the Moon:*
> *The ring around the moon is a light halo that is produced when there are ice crystals present in the earth's upper atmosphere. The halo effect is from moonlight reflecting off the ice crystals and back at the moon."*

The fairies decided to camp on the edge of the meadow for the night. Lying on their little blankets and pillows, they enjoyed a snack of lemon jellybeans and watched the haloed moon as long as they could before drifting off to sleep. Madam Chameleon set her internal clock to wake the young fairies just before sunrise.

They got up a few minutes before dawn, packed up their pillows and blankets, and enjoyed a breakfast of powdered sugar puff pastries and raspberries while they watched the sunrise. The fairies didn't have to worry about the final item on the list because it was right in front of them. An early riser, a girl cyclist, was already in the meadow, not far from the fairies. Her bicycle was leaning up against a tree, and she sat on a blanket spread over the ground, eating an apple and writing in a diary. A Shasta daisy lay next to her on the blanket.

Spiderwort told the others, "The daisy

is one of the flowers of love. We must get a petal to take back to the princess."

Just as she said this, the girl paused in her writing and picked up the daisy. She then began pulling the petals off, reciting, "*He loves me, he loves me not, he loves me...*"

Thinking quickly, Spiderwort said, "We should try to get one of the '*loves me*' petals. Cinnabar, do you think you could distract her while Madam Chameleon slips in, camouflaged, to get the petal?"

Nodding, Cinnabar took off and flew directly in front of the girl. The beautiful, bright red wings were indeed a distraction. The girl stopped plucking petals for a moment as Cinnabar hovered about two feet from her face. Smiling, the girl held out her hand. Cinnabar wasn't afraid and landed on the outstretched palm. The girl looked at the beautiful moth, mesmerized. Cinnabar sat very still and watched Madam Chameleon out of the corner of her eye.

Madam Chameleon had noticed where the last "*loves me*" petal had fallen. As she crept closer, she turned the exact color of the pale green meadow grasses surrounding the petal she sought. When Cinnabar saw that Madam Chameleon had the daisy petal, she took off from the girl's palm.

Cinnabar and Madam Chameleon rejoined the other fairies, and they all laughed and hugged one another. Cinnabar was usually very reserved and quiet; but now, as the other fairies praised her creative bravery, she gave a little curtsey and did a quick ballet pirouette.

Then the fairies flew joyously together, as fast they could, back to the clearing and the tiny princess trapped in the egg of light.

Chapter Seven

Poems

he fairies presented the daisy petal to the princess.

The Spirit of Simplicity was fading in and out more frequently than she had the afternoon before, and the fairies were frightened. The bard and the scarecrow watched her silently.

"Very good," the princess said softly. "Next, you must write two haiku poems. Look in your fairy handbooks to find out exactly what a haiku poem consists of."

The fairies noticed that the ogres were again ignoring them completely. Chaotica and Plethora were now playing hopscotch with some very large river stones that thumped loudly when they were tossed. With each hop, the ground shook like earthquake tremors.

The Princess of Haiku was obviously very clever. By teaching the ogres fun and simple games, she was keeping them from interfering while the fairies worked to break the spell. And the specter and phantom could do nothing about it. No matter how they struggled, the evil spirits couldn't do anything to turn the ogres away from having fun.

As the fairies moved to a quiet corner of the clearing, Spiderwort again read aloud from her handbook:

> "*Haiku: Haiku is the shortest form of poetry. The subject matter of most haiku poems is very simple and can be about anything. In composing a haiku, a poet is cele-*

brating the simple beauty of something, and possibly trying to look at it in a different way than others do, so people reading the poem will appreciate the subject in an original manner. The traditional form of haiku is seventeen syllables divided into three lines. The first line contains five syllables, the second line has seven, and the third line has five. Some traditional haiku subjects include flowers, rainbows, seasons, music, animals, butterflies, leaves, and simple events like falling snow."

"I've written haiku before," said Periwinkle. "I'm in the Big Sisters program, as a little sister, and we did this as one of our activities. I have an idea for a poem. Do you mind if I try one on my own?" The other fairies shook their heads. Periwinkle moved off by herself and engaged in a small discussion with her snail spirit guide.

Meanwhile, Spiderwort, Cinnabar, and Rosemary put their heads together to brainstorm ideas for the second poem. Madam Chameleon stayed off to one side, away from the group, since the children were supposed to compose the poems by themselves.

Spiderwort suggested, "What about tulips for a subject? I just remembered that we forgot to wish Tulip a happy birthday yesterday at Fairy Circle. This could be like a tribute to her, and we could share the poem with her by nut message when our mission is complete."

Cinnabar and Rosemary immediately agreed with their friend's good idea.

"I remember how they taught us to count word syllables in class," Spiderwort added. "You put your hand flat under your chin and speak the words. Every time your chin bumps your hand, you count a syllable."

The others nodded, and the poem composing and chin bumping began.

After fifteen minutes, Periwinkle had finished her poem. She waited patiently for the other three to complete theirs. Then, they all gathered together to recite the poems for Madam Chameleon before addressing the princess. Madam Chameleon was very impressed, and extremely proud of them. She was full of praise.

The princess was waiting expectantly as the fairies approached.

Before reciting her poem, Periwinkle explained to the princess, "I went on an adventure in the spring with my friend, Firefly, as the leader. I admire her very much. We had to find blue moon clover to save black squirrels from a disease brought on by a curse.

"In speaking of the most rare type of blue moon, the last one was six years ago in June. I looked it up. So that was when the clover grew that saved the squirrels.

This poem is in honor of my friend, Firefly, and is a tribute to the wonder and power of the blue moon:

'The rare and glowing
blue moon in June, visits with
fireflies in night skies.'"

There was silence from the group, but the princess, scarecrow, and bard were all smiles.

Next, Rosemary stepped forward to recite the second poem. "This is in honor of our friend, Tulip," she said. "We forgot to wish her a happy birthday yesterday, so I am going to write this poem down when I get home and send it to her by nut message. It's about the daily opening and closing of red tulip flowers:

'Scarlet bowls of day
fold on drowsy pillars green
in night—red tulips.'"

The fairies all watched the princess closely. The tiny spirit's eyes filled with tears and she leaned forward with her face in her hands, weeping silently. After several minutes, she collected herself and looked up at the fairies. With a trembling voice, she breathed two words, very softly. "Simply beautiful."

Chapter Eight

Simple Things

The princess paused for a moment longer, then said, "This brings us to the third and final thing needed to break the spell. A child must give up something important, something that is greatly desired, even treasured."

Spiderwort spoke up immediately. "I just bought a new chess set, but I don't need it. I can use my old one. I will donate the new one to the thrift shop that supports the local homeless shelter."

Periwinkle was fidgeting nervously, anxious to speak next. As soon as Spiderwort finished talking, she said quickly, "I am not going to take pottery classes this year. I want my sister, Megan, to be able to take piano lessons. I have everything I need, and I am the luckiest girl in the world. Not many kids my age get adopted."

Rosemary went next. "I saved up money collecting aluminum cans to buy a season pass to the city water park. I will donate the money to charity instead."

Finally, Cinnabar stepped forward. "I used my birthday money to buy a necklace, but I am going to donate it to our church bazaar coming up next weekend. The proceeds will be going to the local food bank. Also, I am going to donate my video games. I don't really need them. There are a lot of other fun things to do, and playing video games takes time away from my ballet practice anyway."

Barely a second after Cinnabar finished speaking, a sizzling, popping noise was heard, and the egg of light began to break apart. As the egg cracked away, and disappeared completely, the princess was left standing between the scarecrow and the bard.

The ogres stopped playing hopscotch and stared at her.

And the princess said, "I guess the phantom and the specter will be looking for new creatures to inhabit, since they can no longer control the ogres. The spirits won't be able to stand being inside bodies that can experience pleasure from playing simple games."

She was right.

All of a sudden, the ogres began holding their heads as if in pain, and nasty green vapors started streaming out of their eyes and ears. The wisps of vapor took shape in front of the ogres. The Phantom of Excess was lumpy and fat, and the Specter of Pandemonium was long and thin. They were both a sickly green color; and the nasty, stringy vapor they were made

of was churning and writhing. Everyone in the clearing felt seasick looking at them.

The ogres didn't waste any time leaving once they were free of the evil spirits. Even though Chaotica and Plethora were not very nice creatures themselves, it had not been fun all these years with that extra ugliness inside of them. The sisters quickly snatched up the coconuts and river stones and stomped off through the forest.

The phantom and specter moved closer to the princess. As the nasty spirits neared, the bard and scarecrow stepped protectively in front of her, and the fairies all raised their wands to defend themselves if necessary. But the princess told the fairies, "They cannot hurt us. We are too strong for them."

The evil spirits lingered only a few seconds longer before turning to go, spitting and hissing as they left. "Dratted fairies!"

The princess, bard, and scarecrow all thanked the fairies for their help. And the princess told them, "As long as one person on earth can enjoy simple things, I will

always exist. Please try to keep my spirit alive." Then, hand in hand, the three friends walked away together into the forest, disappearing into the morning mist.

At home the next day, each of the girls carried out their promises, giving away treasured belongings and giving up desires.

Madam Chameleon sent nut messages to Madam Toad and several other fairy mentors to announce their success.

Rosemary carefully wrote down the red tulip poem and sent it in a walnut to Tulip, wishing her a belated birthday and telling her about the adventure.

Cinnabar finally read her message from James. He had invited her on a picnic and suggested that she ask her mentor if it could be arranged. She spent some time that day wording a response to her new friend, thanking him again for his help, and telling him that she would contact Madam Finch to see if they could set up a picnic.

Periwinkle talked to her parents and told them she wanted to wait a few years before taking pottery lessons. She had

Simple and Free Fun Things To Do

1. Fly a kite.

2. Blow bubbles. Make bubble blowing solution from soap and water.

3. Play string games like cat's cradle.

4. Put on a play in the back-yard with your friends.

5. Draw sidewalk or driveway chalk pictures!

plenty of other things to keep her busy, and she really wanted to concentrate on doing well in school.

Spiderwort spent her free time working in the garden, skating, helping to look after her little brother, and playing word games.

In addition to all of these things, she began brainstorming a long list of ideas for a new brochure she was going to write: *Simple and Free Fun Things to Do*. While she scribbled the list of ideas, she thought how interesting the first three days of summer break had been. And she wondered what other adventures might await her and her fairy friends over the next two months.

The End

Fairy Fun

Haikus
by J. H. Sweet

Exit Sign
Four lit green letters
awaiting our departure
proud of their success.

Peacock
Screaming eyes of light,
on stone hearts and souls reflect
peacock feathered bright.

Grand Piano
Carved wood painted black
openly awaiting touch
to steal the silence.

Write your own haiku!

Using the information from the fairy handbook, write a haiku poem for one of the following subjects: redbird, cartwheel, puppies, toothbrush, milk, clouds, peppermint, pearl, screen door, button, flag, ice cream, butterfly, jumprope, kitten, popcorn, sidewalk cracks, bald eagle, feather, bare feet, kite, mom's purse, ribbon, cotton candy.

If you don't feel like writing a poem, perhaps spend some of your free time drawing sidewalk chalk pictures, riding a bicycle, skating, walking a dog, jumping rope, or learning to play chess.

FAIRY FACTS

Lose Yourself in a World of Kings and Knights

The game of chess, featuring kings, bishops, pawns, knights, and rooks, is anything but medieval fantasy. Chess is a game of strategy and an exercise in ultimate brainpower with opponents striving to outthink and outmaneuver one another. Widely thought to have its origins in sixth-century India, the original game was quite different from the modern version and included pieces such as an elephant and a ship. Oddly enough, the queen, which is the most powerful of the current chess game pieces, was not even part of the original game. Many variations of chess have been played throughout the centuries in various countries, including one played on a circular game board. The television series Star Trek was responsible for the invention of a multi-level version of the game called Tri-Dimensional Chess.

Bobcats

Bobcats are small wildcats, usually weighing no more than twenty pounds. They have short tails and live mainly in the American Southwest. Bobcats live in both rocky and wooded habitats. They like to eat small animals such as rabbits and squirrels, but they sometimes kill and eat larger animals like pigs and deer.

The Scarecrow

What is the purpose of scarecrows? Well, it is really all in the name, isn't it? Scare crow. Since the very first people started raising crops there has always been a need to scare crows away at night. Once the sun goes down, crows like to gather in large groups, often more than thirty crows at a time, and not only will they eat away at the crop's fallen seeds but they will also make a whole lot of noise! And, worst of all, crows like to gather in the same place night after night. Can you imagine thirty loud birds outside your window causing a racket all night, every night? Not anyone's idea of fun. So, at some point scarecrows were invented to keep the crows away. Generally a scarecrow is a large stick put in the ground with another stick crossing it. Clothes and stuffing are then added to the sticks to make the two sticks look like a person. However, some farmers take pride in their scarecrows and they spend a lot of time and energy making them look like people. Scarecrows exist all over the world and even pop up in mythology from England to Japan!

Inside you is the power to do anything

. . . the adventures continue

Firefly and her friends are going on a camping adventure. But little do they know that they are about to be sent on a real adventure, where the stakes are nothing less than the future of all the species on Earth.

The black squirrel looked nervous. When he spoke, his soft voice quavered a little at first. "I have made a long journey to be here because a terrible sickness has struck several black squirrel colonies in the far North, and it is spreading. The sickness causes death."

The black squirrel stopped his story for a moment. When he started speaking again, his voice shook. "But I haven't told you the worst part. The curse is a *Calendar-Chain Curse,* set up to attack a new species each month. Next month, all white-tailed deer will die. In May, beavers, and the following month, earthworms. In July, snow geese, and so on. Eventually, it will reach humans. There is no stopping it." He sighed, "It is a *perfect curse.*"

This is a very dangerous mission, and Madam Toad is dispatching some of her best fairies: Firefly, Thistle, Marigold, and their new friend Periwinkle. The girls will have to use all of their magic, brains, and brawn to stop the perfect curse!

Come visit us at fairychronicles.com

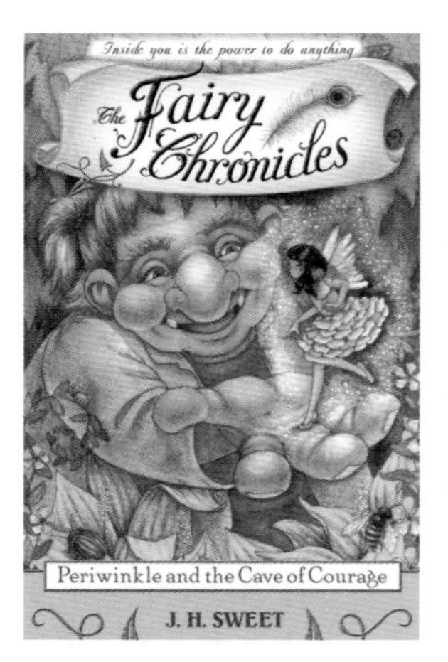

Fairies always work well together, but what happens when they have to lead a team made up of many different kinds of magical creatures?

"I have been instructed to tell you of a challenge we must all participate in," continued Madam Toad. "Not far from here lies the entrance to the Cave of Courage. The Cave of Courage produces courage for all of mankind. Every one hundred years, the cave must be recharged. This is done by an organized team effort between magical creatures. For this recharging,

Mother Nature has chosen a dwarf, a leprechaun, a gnome, a troll, two brownies, and four fairies to participate."

With four fairies involved, no challenge is too difficult, but now they must rely on the help of others, something that not everyone does well...

Come visit us at fairychronicles.com

Cinnabar and the Island of Shadows

A shadow is a person's closest companion. Shadows protect and guide the humans they are attached to. But what if you were born without a shadow?

Madam Toad paused before she continued. "Human shadows are unlike any other shadows on earth. They are much different from animal, mountain, plant, cloud, insect, and building shadows. For starters, human shadows are much more complex. And they are the only shadows that are magically constructed. Human shadows are manufactured by shadowmakers on the Island of Shadows, and are delivered to children shortly after their births by hawks that work for the shadowmakers."

"Today, Mother Nature has discovered that seven children in various countries of the world have not received their shadows."

And so Cinnabar, Mimosa, Dewberry, and Spiderwort must travel to the Island of Shadows, confront the King and Queen of that remarkable place, discover what happened to these seven shadows and, worst of all, find out if there might be someone or something behind it all!

Come visit us at fairychronicles.com

About the Author

J. H. Sweet has always looked for the magic in the everyday. She has an imaginary dog named Jellybean Ebenezer Beast. Her hobbies include hiking, photography, knitting, and basketry. She also enjoys watching a variety of movies and sports. Her favorite superhero is her husband, with Silver Surfer coming in a close second. She loves many of the same things the fairies love, including live oak trees, mockingbirds, weathered terra-cotta, butterflies, bees, and cypress knees. In the fairy game of "If I were a jellybean, what flavor would I be?" she would be green apple. J. H. Sweet lives with her husband in South Texas and has a degree in English from Texas State University.

About the Illustrator

Holly Sierra's illustrations are visually enchanting with particular attention to decorative, mystical, and multicultural themes. Holly received her fine arts education at SUNY Purchase in New York and lives in Myrtle Beach with her husband, Steve, and their three children, Gabrielle, Esme, and Christopher.